PANDA MAN to the RESCUE!

STORY by SHO MAKURA   ART by HARUHI KATO

Meet Panda Man, the greatest martial artist in the world.

That may not be quite true, but Panda Man thinks so, and that's what matters.

Every day, deep in the mountains, Panda Man puts himself through a rigorous training routine.

Would you look at that! Today's training has already begun. Let's watch.

First Panda Man punches his punching bag 100 times. Then he lifts weights 200 times.

Finally, he sharpens his mind by sitting under the rushing water of an icy-cold waterfall.

Waving his arm with all his might, Panda Man ran full force toward a nearby log.

Unbelievable!

Can Panda Man really chop through the log with his bare hands?

Apparently not.

But wait! Panda Man managed to break the log after all! Cowvin applauded wildly.

Then he grew serious.

"Mr. Panda Man," he said. "I didn't just come to see your super-strength. A ruthless band of thieves is attacking my village! You're the only one in the world who can stop them!"

"Boing?" Panda Man replied. "A band of thieves? Oooh, that makes me mad! The world's maddest! These cowards need a dose of justice. The world's justest justice. Yes. I, Panda Man, will save your village!"

Of course, there was a catch.

"I must warn you," Panda Man continued. "My services don't come cheap. My fee will be... one *million* dollars!"

Poor Cowvin.
Poor, poor little shorthorn.

"One...m-million...?" Cowvin gasped. "Our village can't afford that much."

"It's nothing personal." Panda Man shrugged. "I just make it a point to be the world's most... well, everything. So I have to have the world's most expensive protection fees. I have no choice."

Suddenly, Cowvin had an idea.

"Hey! I have an idea! My sister Moona is really famous for making the world's yummiest butter cake. If you helped my village, you could eat all the butter cake you want!"

"Did you say the world's *yummiest* butter cake?" Panda Man asked. "In that case, I'll waive my fee...just this once."

And since they visited so many of Panda Man's favorite world-famous sites, for Cowvin, their trip became the world's longest.

Finally, Panda Man and Cowvin
arrived in New Milk Village.

But something wasn't right.

All of the townsfolk had fallen to the ground! Cowvin's sister was somewhere among them.

WH...WHAT HAPPENED?! WHERE'S MOONA?! HAS ANYONE SEEN HER?

"Oh, Cowvin... You did it!" Moona cried, rising slowly to her hooves. "You found Mr. Panda Man! But I'm afraid you're too late."

"What happened, Moona?" Cowvin asked.

"Well, we had just begun the day's milking when...

21

...those awful thieves showed up!"

Moona explained that the chief thief was a spicy-food-loving lion named Leo Pepperpot.

"He attacked us with seasoning!" Moona cried.

"All right, all right already," Panda Man said. "I'm here, so you have nothing to fear. But before I do anything, I must have a taste of the world's yummiest butter cake!"

Just thinking about the cake made Panda Man drool.

HOW TO MAKE BUTTER

FWISH

FWISH

Cows' "milk" is really a mixture of milk and cream. Separate the cream and it can be whipped into butter!

①

DWOOP

②

"B...butter cake...?" Moona gasped. "But, Mr. Panda Man, butter is made with cream. And since Leo Pepperpot has taken all of our milk..."

OH NO! YOU MEAN...

Poor Panda Man.
This was more than
he could bear.

The shock made him
dizzy. His eyes went
blank, and he fell to
the ground.

As Panda Man sprang to attention, his eyes burned with rage. Rage over the butter cake, mind you, not the great injustice that the villagers had suffered.

But...let's just keep that to ourselves.

Panda Man's passion moved the villagers to tears.

With the hope of the whole village behind him—and the promise of butter cake in front of him—Panda Man went off in search of the thieves.

35

A moment later, Panda Man was extremely bored. To pass the time, he told himself a story.

Use these images to create a story of your own!

FISH

PANCAKE

DUSTPAN

CHESTNUT

SQUID

CHIPMUNK

KICK

SWEET POTATO

CRAB

SLIPPERS

MOON

NINJA

UNDERPANTS

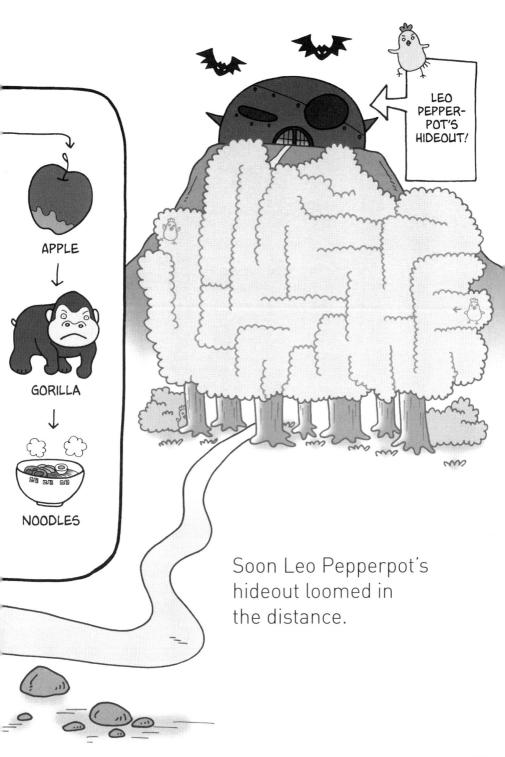

APPLE

↓

GORILLA

↓

NOODLES

LEO PEPPER-POT'S HIDEOUT!

Soon Leo Pepperpot's hideout loomed in the distance.

And inside Leo Pepperpot's den, Panda Man was being watched.

Leave it to Leo to make things difficult.

How are Panda Man and Cowvin going to get past that dragon?

IT'S HUGE!

AND THAT TAIL! IT GOES ON FOREVER!

WHOA. LET'S... STAY AWAY FROM HIS TAIL.

RIGHT! TOUCHING IT IS SURE TO WAKE HIM UP!

EXIT

43

Panda Man unleashed **the world's loudest sneeze!**

45

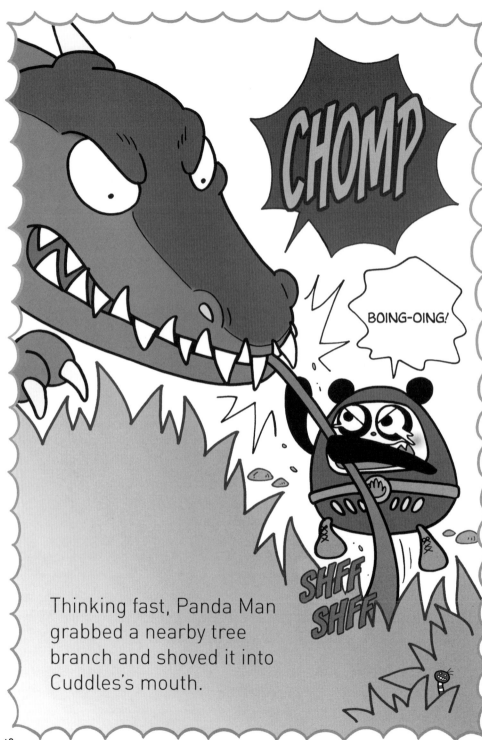

Thinking fast, Panda Man grabbed a nearby tree branch and shoved it into Cuddles's mouth.

Pirate Puss was making copies of himself!

And if Panda Man didn't do something fast, he'd soon have a **pirate platoon** on his hands!

"Mr. Panda Man! We have to find the original Pirate Puss!"

Panda Man and Cowvin need your help!

Look at the drawing below and find its match!

Original Pirate Puss

He might not be in the same pose. Then again, he might.

Panda Man flung himself into the center of the pirates.

Now there was nothing standing between Panda Man and the terrible Leo Pepperpot!

63

"Since you've made it this far, I'll let you in on my top secret plan," Leo smirked. "Inside this rocket is all the milk from New Milk Village."

"All of it?" Panda Man asked.

"*All* of it," Leo replied.

"What are you—"

"Stop interrupting me," Leo snapped, "and I'll tell you my plan."

"Ever since I was a little boy, I've hated milk. No matter how I cried, my mother made me drink the stuff every day. 'But it's *good* for you,' she said. 'Good for the *bones*.' Rubbish."

GRRRRR

I SWORE THAT SOMEDAY
I WOULD RID THE WORLD
OF MILK FOR GOOD! AND
NOW THAT I'VE FINISHED
THIS ROCKET, MY PLAN IS
ALMOST COMPLETE.

Hearing Leo's dastardly plan made Panda Man and Cowvin piping mad!

Without warning, Leo aimed his cannon at Panda Man and fired.

Cowvin ran to his side, but Panda Man's eyes were blank. He didn't move.

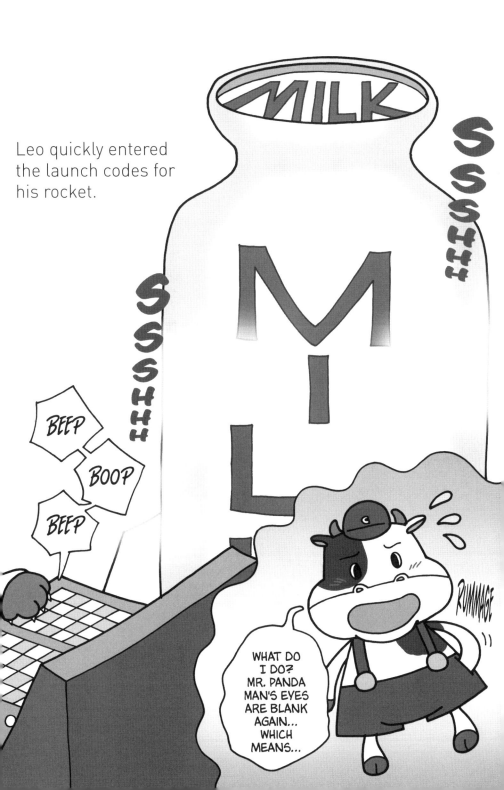

Cowvin took a pencil from his pocket and...

TOK

Panda Man was back!

With his eyes restored, he sprang into action.

He flung off his shoe and attacked.

Well, how about that! Panda Man might just
be the world's greatest martial artist after all.

The Milk Rocket raced skyward with Panda Man holding on for dear life. There wasn't much else he could do.

Did Leo win this fight?
Was this the end of milk?!

Never more afraid in all his life, Panda Man farted.

Not just any fart. The world's longest, strongest, most fartiest fart.

The sheer force of Panda Man's personal wind sent the Milk Rocket spinning.

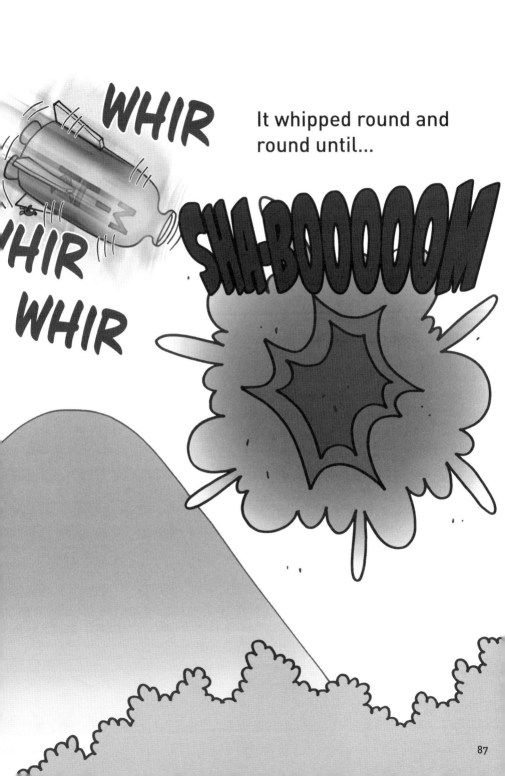

WHIR

WHIR

WHIR

It whipped round and round until...

SHA-BOOOOOM!

The Milk Rocket's spinning turned the milk into a great glob of butter. The rocket exploded right over New Milk Village, dropping the butter smack-dab in the middle of town.

BLOOP

Cowvin and the villagers ran to their fallen hero.

And what a hero he was. He had defeated Leo Pepperpot and saved New Milk Village, assuring milk lovers everywhere that they would never be without their milk!

THANK YOU, MR. PANDA MAN!! HOW CAN WE EVER REPAY YOU?!

There was only one way for the villagers to repay Panda Man. With the giant glob of butter they made the world's largest and yummiest butter cake!

Panda Man opened his mouth wide—wider than anyone in the world—and...

There goes Panda Man, the world's greatest hero. Strong. Heroic. Brave. Wherever there's evil to defeat and good food to eat, he'll be there.

Farewell, Panda Man!
Until we meet again!

Panda Man to the Rescue!

VIZ Kids Edition

Story by Sho Makura
Art by Haruhi Kato

Translation: Katherine Schilling
Rewriting: Deric Hughes
Touch-up Art & Lettering: John Hunt
Graphics & Cover Design: Frances O. Liddell
Editor: Traci N. Todd

VP, Production: Alvin Lu
VP, Sales & Product Marketing: Gonzalo Ferreyra
VP, Creative: Linda Espinosa
Publisher: Hyoe Narita

BOYO-YON PANDARU-MAN
© 2008 by Sho Makura, Haruhi Kato
All rights reserved.
First published in Japan in 2008 by SHUEISHA Inc., Tokyo.
English translation rights arranged by SHUEISHA Inc.

Printed in China

Published by VIZ Media, LLC
P.O. Box 77010
San Francisco, CA 94107

10 9 8 7 6 5 4 3 2 1
First printing, October 2010

www.vizkids.com